Annie and Snowball
and the
Magical House

The Seventh Book of Their Adventures

Cynthia Rylant

Illustrated by Suçie Stevenson

READY-TO-READ

SIMON SPOTLIGHT

New York   London   Toronto   Sydney

For Peter Stevenson
and Naomi King
—S. S.

SIMON SPOTLIGHT
An imprint of Simon & Schuster Children's Publishing Division
1230 Avenue of the Americas, New York, New York 10020
Text copyright © 2010 by Cynthia Rylant
Illustrations copyright © 2010 by Suçie Stevenson
All rights reserved, including the right of reproduction in whole or in part in any form.
SIMON SPOTLIGHT, READY-TO-READ,
and colophon are registered trademarks of Simon & Schuster, Inc.
For information about special discounts for bulk purchases, please contact
Simon & Schuster Special Sales at 1-866-506-1949 or business@simonandschuster.com.
Also available in a Simon Spotlight hardcover edition.
Designed by Tom Daly
The text of this book was set in Goudy.
The illustrations for this book were rendered in pen-and-ink and watercolor.
Manufactured in the United States of America 0211 LAK
First Simon Spotlight paperback edition March 2011
2 4 6 8 10 9 7 5 3 1
The Library of Congress has cataloged the hardcover edition as follows:
Rylant, Cynthia.
Annie and Snowball and the magical house / Cynthia Rylant;
illustrated by Suçie Stevenson.—1st ed.
p. cm. — (Ready-to-read)
Summary: Annie takes her rabbit to the home of her new friend Sarah
and enjoys seeing the pretty house full of frilly things, walking in the beautiful garden,
and making a tiny garden house for a fairy tea party.
ISBN 978-1-4169-3945-0 (hc)
[1. Friendship—Fiction. 2. Play—Fiction.] I. Stevenson, Suçie, ill.
II. Title.
PZ7.R982Annm 2010
[E]—dc22
2009012089
ISBN 978-1-4169-3949-8 (pb)

Contents

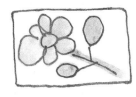

A New Friend

At school Annie made a new friend.
Her friend's name was Sarah.
One day Sarah invited Annie
over to play.

5

Sarah said that Annie could even bring
her bunny, Snowball.

After school, Annie asked her dad
if she could play at Sarah's house.
"Sure!" said her dad, and he drove
her there.

Sarah's house looked like
a gingerbread cottage.
"Wow," said Annie.
"I like Sarah's house."

8

"I bet someone bakes
a lot of cookies here,"
said Annie's dad.

He knocked on the door.
When it opened, Sarah was there
with her mother.

Sarah's mother was very friendly.
She invited Annie and her dad
and Snowball inside.
"Wow," said Annie.

Sarah's house was just *full* of frilly things.
And frilly things were Annie's
favorite things.

12

"I like your lamps and your teacups
and your flowery chairs," said Annie.

13

"Thank you," said Sarah's mother with a smile. "Sarah and I enjoy being dainty."
"Me too," said Annie.

Sarah's mother gave Annie's dad
a plate of sparkle cookies.

She told him she would bring
Annie home in time for dinner.
Annie's dad was very happy
with his cookies.

When he left, Annie said to Sarah,
"So what shall we do now?"
Sarah smiled.
"I have an idea," she said.

Fairy Tea

Sarah took Annie into the garden.

"It's so pretty!" said Annie.

The garden had rows of roses and climbing vines and walls of ivy and lovely stone angels.

19

"I love it here," said Annie.

"Would you like to make a fairy house?"
asked Sarah.

"Fairies like to have tea parties.
And they need a special garden house
just for fairy tea," Sarah said.

Annie smiled.

Already she was having so much fun.

Snowball was having fun, too.

She was nibbling some lavender.

Sarah and Annie searched
for a perfect spot for fairy tea.
They found one
under the large green leaves
of a hosta plant.

"It's perfect," said Sarah.
"Nice and private," said Annie.
Then they set about
making the fairy house.

Annie found pieces of walnut shells
the squirrels had left behind.
The shells would make perfect chairs.

Sarah found a nice smooth stone
for a tea table.

Together they made walls
from small rocks, and they
placed rose petals on top
to make them pretty.

The girls found small red berries
and tiny green pebbles
and little bits of violet.

They found bird feathers
and tiny pinecones.

30

And they found a bit of bark
with a hole in its center.
It was perfect for a fairy door.

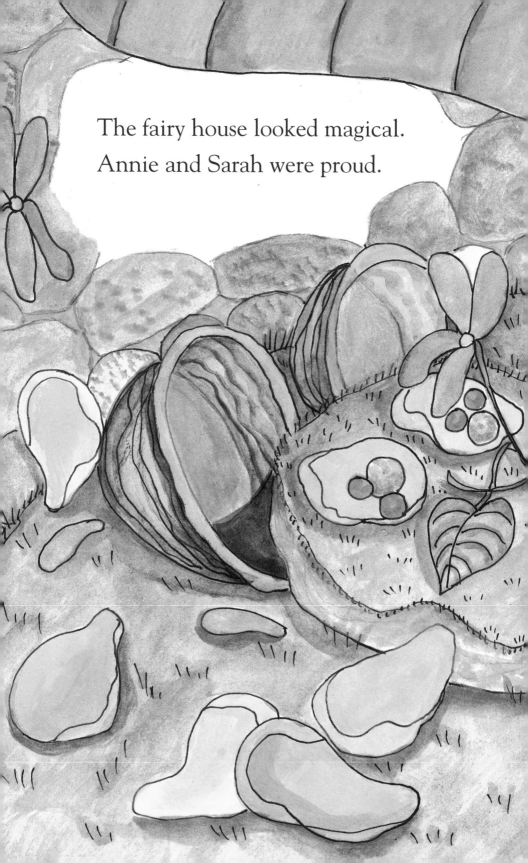

The fairy house looked magical.
Annie and Sarah were proud.

"I wish the fairies would invite us
for tea," said Annie.

"Maybe someday they will." Sarah smiled.

"In the meantime would you like
some cookies and milk?"

"Yes!" said Annie.
She blew a rose petal off Snowball's nose
and followed Sarah inside.

Home

When Annie arrived home,
she had a frilly hanky
that Sarah's mother had given her
and a handful of radishes for Snowball.

"Are there any sparkle cookies left?"
Annie asked her dad.
"Oops," said Annie's dad.
Annie smiled.

"That's okay," she said.
"I already had cookies and milk."

"Me too," said Annie's dad, smiling back.
"Did you have fun at Sarah's house?"
he asked.

Annie thought about the garden
and the fairy house and all
of the fairy tea parties to come.
She nodded her head.
"Yes," she said. "It was *magical*."